Ernest Warburton Shurtleff

The New Year's peace, and other poems

Ernest Warburton Shurtleff

The New Year's peace, and other poems

ISBN/EAN: 9783337222611

Printed in Europe, USA, Canada, Australia, Japan

Cover: Foto ©Andreas Hilbeck / pixelio.de

More available books at **www.hansebooks.com**

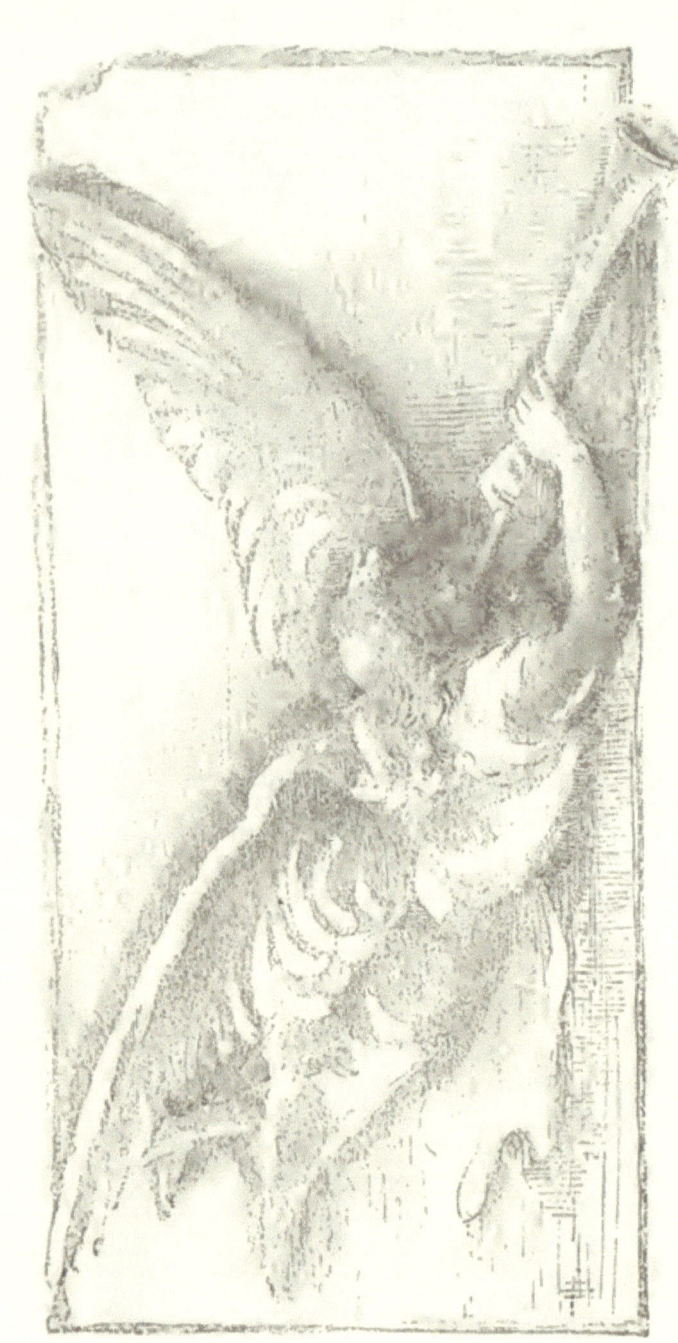

"And, hark! seraphic sounds I hear
Of soulful music light." — PAGE 9.

THE
NEW YEAR'S PEACE

And Other Poems

BY

ERNEST WARBURTON SHURTLEFF

ILLUSTRATED

BOSTON
D. LOTHROP AND COMPANY
32 FRANKLIN STREET

CONTENTS.

5

6

THE NEW YEAR'S PEACE.

I saw the portals of the dawning year
    Thrown open to the light.
I saw pale Time, a hoary king, appear,
With crown of flashing crystals, cold and clear,
    Shining upon his wintry locks of white.

He raised his quiet, earnest eyes to Heaven,
    The east bloomed into day.
"O world!" he cried, "the Old Year is forgiven!
Her sins, that fell like bitter raindrops driven
    On stormy seas, shall rise no more for aye!"

Then January, with a childish grace,
    And merry song, arose;
And with her robes, that shone like frosted lace,
And smiles as bright as sunshine on her face,
    Stood like an angel, purer than the snows.

7

I saw her tarry at the poor man's door;
   Her merry greeting rang
Like music through his cottage, and once more
His heart grew light — more light than e'er before —
   And, lifting up his face to God, he sang.

I saw her kiss poor tear-worn cheeks, and bring
   Light to the mourner's eyes;
I saw the sad turn from their pain, and sing;
I saw the weary bathe in Hope's pure spring —
   That sweet Siloam that flows from Paradise.

O January, month of joy! we hear
   On every side thy voice;
It fills our spirits with its life and cheer.
The future waits for all men bright and clear,
   Each rising sun cries to the world, "*Rejoice!*"

He treasures not our sins who rules in Heaven.
   Time, with an angel pen,
Each daybreak writes that one sweet word, "*Forgiven,*"
On every heart that for the right has striven;
   And peace, like snow, makes pure the paths of men.

8

ON CHRISTMAS MORNING.

THE storms have flocked through heav'n's high hall,
  Like birds on wings of snow,
And let their frosty plumage fall
  Along the hills below.
And now the tide of Christmas morn
  In eastern skies rolls higher,
Till every shrub and wayside thorn
  Seems touched with wondrous fire.
What visions in the light I see
  Like heavenly hosts of old!
The sunbeams walk my path with me
  Like angels clad in gold.
They throng the hills, the open sky,
  The zenith seems aglow
With shining garments trailing by
  Of blue and gold and snow.

And, hark! seraphic sounds I hear
  Of soulful music light,
As though some angel, passing near,
  Had touched me in his flight,

9

And by that touch, so near divine,
    Soft as of snow-bird's wings,
Had quickened every sense of mine
    To know of heavenly things.
" Hail! Christ the Lord is born again!"
    The bright host seems to sing.
" His birth is in the hearts of men;
    Ring, bells of Christmas, ring!"
And then the joyful swaying bells
    Their sweetest music play,
And down the hills the echo tells
    The tidings to the day.

My Saviour, while I listen here,
    And view these glories break,
Come Thou, my needy life draw near,
    And me Thy subject make!
Oh, let my heart, with peace untold,
    Thy humble cradle be!
A manger gave Thee rest of old —
    Come now and dwell with me!
And on this lowly life of mine,
    Where pain and strivings are,
From out of Heaven a joy shall shine
    Like Bethlehem's second star.

Each gladdened thought, on bended knee,
    No more to stray or err,
Shall bring true praise and love to Thee
    For frankincense and myrrh.

A holy meaning so shall fill
    The beauty of the day.
A living joy the heart shall thrill
    No more to pass away.
New songs shall echo from the bells
    That usher in the morn,
And light shall fill the soul where dwells
    The infant Christ new-born.
"His birth is in the hearts of men!"
    So shall the spirit sing,
"And Bethlehem's star has dawned again;
    Ring, bells of Christmas, ring!"

SONG OF YEARS.

THE years have songs to cheer, they have glad voices,
    They have sweet smiles that bright as sunbeams burn;
But even while the listening ear rejoices,
    They speed away and never more return!

God rains the moments down like golden showers.
 We gather them, and lo! they are but dew.
They melt like flakes of snow, they fade like flowers,
 Or glittering stars on morning's brightening blue.

Ah, me! the golden fancies that have perished,
 And left behind but footprints of their cheer!
Some autumn falls on every summer cherished;
 Each laughing day ends with a dewy tear!
Yet will I not for years departed sorrow;
 The gentle lesson of the bright to-day
Shall be my key to ope the fair to-morrow,
 When Night's cold tear in smiles is charmed away.
Be glad, O soul! sing not a mournful story!
 Hope, like a sun, awakes the future's dawn.
The Past shall live again, where, bathed in glory,
 Through Death's hushed hall, God's angel becks us
  on!

12

WINGÈD WORDS.

THE words that our spirits utter,
  Like birds, speed far away,
And some sing on forever,
  In the realms of endless day;

But some are lost in darkness,
  And tell of sorrow and pain,
And the music is low and mournful
  That steals from their soft refrain.

Ah, happy he whose spirit
  Hath sent sweet birds away!
Their thrilling notes shall charm him
  Through all that endless day.

But alas for him whose spirit
　　Hath given no sweetness birth,
When the dearest songs of heaven
　　Are the songs conceived on earth!

'TWAS VIOLET TIME.

'Twas violet time when he and she
Went roaming the meadows wide and free.
　　A happy lad and lass were they,
　　Their hearts, their hopes, their voices **gay** —
She seventeen, he twenty-three.

The skies were calm as a sleeping sea,
And the hills and streams and the mossy lea
A part of the wooing seemed to be —
　　　　　·'Twas violet time.

Years fled, and weak and old grew he;
His form was bent like a snow-bowed tree,
　　His hair was white, and hers was gray,
　　But their hearts were young as a morn in **May**,
And in their souls — sweet mystery! —
　　　　　'Twas violet time!

A SONG OF LIFE.

I saw in dreams that Kingdom blest
    That opens through Immortal Day;
And in its quiet bourn of rest,
    Beside the angel-trodden way,
I found three bright ones weaving strands
    Of sunlight into fabrics rare,
That glistened in their busy hands
    Like rainbows blent with golden air.

"Pray tell me, lovely ones," I cried,
    "What costly raiment have ye there?
Shall kings, or monarchs glorified,
    Those robes through lands celestial wear?"

Their shining brows the weavers raised,
    And on me turned their sinless view;
And while with silent awe I gazed,
    Their words came sweet as fall of dew:

15

" Nay, not for those whom men adore
   Our costly work is wrought," they said,
" But for the needy, weak, and poor,
   That dwell on earth uncomforted!"

" The heavenly plan is just," I cried;
   And, turning back to life's great tide,
I felt the gladdening truth anew,
   That man on earth this work may do.

Oh, people! ye whose arms are strong,
   Uplift the weak, their cause uphold.
God's kingdoms to His poor belong.
   Earth gives the rich their gates of gold.

And ye who wield the gifted pen,
   Go write the simple tidings down.
The blessing of your fellow-men
   Is sweeter than the world's renown.
Go serve thy neighbor well, and when
   Thou diest thou shalt have thy crown.

No shining day was ever done
   That brightened not its own sweet even;
No noble life whose sinking sun
   Oped not bright vistas into Heaven.

16

ON HER BIRTHDAY.

Her years steal by like birds through cloudless skies,
    Soft singing as they go ;
She views their flight with sunshine in her eyes,
    She hears their music low,
And on her forehead, beautiful and wise,
    Shines love's most holy glow.

There is no pain for her in Time's soft flight.
    Her spirit is so fair
Her days shine as they pass her, in the light
    Her gentle doings wear ;
On her fair brow I never saw the night,
    But Hope's glad star shone there.

It is a blessing just to see her face
    Pass like an angel's by —
Her soft brown hair, sweet eyes, and lips that grace
    The smiles that round them lie ;
The brightest sunbeam in its heavenly place
    Might joy to catch her eye.

Dear life that groweth sweeter growing old!
   I bring this verse to thee,
A tiny flower, but in its heart the gold
   Of lasting love from me;
While in my soul that deeper love I hold
   Too great for man to see.

THY HOUSE IS DUST.

THY house is dust.   All this which men behold
Is thy soul's dwelling shaped from nature's mold.
   This stately beauty of thy marble brow,
   This queenly grace before which others bow,
These ringlets shining on thy neck like gold —
They are but petals to thy life, and fold
Thy soul like some poor glow-worm from the cold.
   When Death comes, he will gently teach thee how
      Thy house is dust.

Men have thy brow with glory aureoled,
Thy name among the beautiful enrolled;
   But wilt thou be in Heaven what thou art now?
   Take heed thy dust be not more fair than thou,
For thou must leave it when thy days are told —
      Thy house is dust.

PROPHECIES.

THE tender buds are prophecies of flowers.
  The hidden germs that wake
Beneath the kisses of the morning showers,
  And into color break,
Will some time in the golden summer hours
  Bright-petaled blossoms make.
It needs no seer these simple truths to tell,
For in the seeds the coming blossoms dwell.

The four smooth eggs that in the oriole's nest
  Like dainty jewels lie,
Close-pressed beneath the patient mother's breast,
  Will, e'er the month speed by,
Give woodland minstrels blithe and gayly dressed
  To charm the open sky.
It needs no sage to speak these simple words,
The eggs themselves are prophecies of birds.

So all the shining world of nature through
  We read the end of things.
We know what birds shall cleave the welkin blue
  With music on their wings,
What flowers shall ope their lips to drink the dew
  Of night's refreshing springs.
We read of summer in the early May,
And see to-morrow's image in to-day.

O friend, so let me prophesy for thee!
  Not by the wizard's art,
Whose vain imaginings are wild and free
  As foolish Fancy's heart,
Nor by the wonders of astrology
  In night's star-written chart;
But from thine own glad nature, young and fair,
And by the promise that is written there.

I see for thee a summer in the spring,
  I see the coming flowers,
I see that thou wilt teach sad hearts to sing,
  And bring them happy hours.
I see the sunshine — Day's great golden wing —
  O'erspread home's pleasant bowers,
To rest about thy life in coming years
With not a cloud but what its rainbow wears.

How do I know such sweet things to disclose?
  'Tis only what I read.
How do I know a bud shall be a rose,
  And not a common weed?
How do I know the purest flower that grows
  Sleeps in the lily's seed?
Why prophesy for them and not for thee,
When in thy life so much for hope I see!

I do not say no storm-days shall be thine,
  No shadows with the light,
Because all kinds of weather must combine
  To make a blossom bright.
I only say more joys shall come to shine
  Than sorrows come to blight.
I only say that in thy life to-day
I read this sunshine for the far away.

THE NIGHT IS DEAD.

THE night is dead, and the day is come!
  A child trips singing through the dew.
Her face by the dawn is flushed with bloom,
  She goes to play when the night is through.

A child trips singing through the dew,
  But the web is changed on Time's swift loom, —
A bride is wed, and the morn breaks blue;
  The night is dead, and the day is come.

The web is changed on Time's swift loom,
  'Tis the end of life's long retinue;
A white head rests in the twilight gloom —
  The kindest sleep e'er mortal knew.

'Tis the end of life's long retinue,
  Yet an angel stands in God's high Home;
Eternity enwraps her view —
  The night is dead, and the day is come!

THE BELL-RINGER AND THE ANGELS.

THE aged bellman climbed his lonely tower,
  Where cooed the doves, each to its gentle mate.
Day's rosy footprints faded with the hour,
  And shadows gathered at the chapel gate.

The years had crowned with white the old man's brow,
  And from his life his dearest joys had flown;
The friends his hearth had cheered were dead, and now
  Of all his kindred he was left alone.

His mellow bell the death of evening tolled,
  O'er listening wood and glen the music rung;
Then night's blue gates were sealed with stars of gold,
  And Beauty watched in heaven with silent tongue.

Soon, like a spirit of the quiet hour,
  From eastern dreams the smiling moon arose,
And through the lonely chapel's fretted tower
  The slanting beams streamed in like silver snows.

25

The bellman tarried, gazing on the night;
    He thought of all his kindred gone to rest;
He longed to view them in their glory bright,
    And clasp again his children to his breast.

He thought of Easter's risen Lord.   He thought
    Of Mary weeping at her Master's feet;
And from his lips the prayer his mother taught
    Fell like an echo of his childhood sweet.

When lo! two angels, clad in beauty rare,
    Beside him stood, more bright than song can tell.
Pure thoughts of God had made their features fair,
    And blessings from their lips like music fell.

The wondering bellman raised his trembling hand
    To shield his eyes, with glory dimmed and dazed.
" Oh, speak! " he cried, " from what celestial land
    Have ye descended?"   Spelled with joy, he gazed

Upon their shining brows, their gentle eyes;
    And, as their quiet answer charmed his ear,
He felt his joyous soul within him rise,
    Glad as a bird that finds its freedom near.

26

" We are the angels Life and Death," they sung.
   " Choose thou between us, which shall be thy guide."
Dumb for a moment was the bellman's tongue,
   Then, with a sudden thrill of joy, he cried:

" What! Life and *Death!* I thought that Death was
         drear;
   I thought he came with sorrow in his breath —
But lo! ye both so mild, so bright, appear,
   I know not which is Life or which is Death!"

Then forth he stretched his trembling arm, and took
   The nearer angel's shining garment-hem;
For in his eyes he saw a gentle look
   That 'minded him of Christ of Bethlehem.

The angel smiled, and he the smile returned;
   " Art thou not Life?" he asked, with eager breath.
" Not so," the angel spake; "yet thou hast earned
   Through me immortal joys; lo! I am Death."
         .   .   .   .   .

Night hurried on. The stars of morning gray
   Grew dim; and in the east pale colors played.
The bellman's spirit passed that night away
   To wear the crown his life on earth had made.

And this is dying. That which man calls Death
  Not as a dark and fearful shadow comes ;
It is an angel mild, with loving breath,
  That does God's gentle bidding in our homes.

AT THE GATE.

I.

A SINGER stood at Heaven's gate,
  And gazed in through the shining bars.
The night was hushed, the hour was late,
  And Beauty dreamed among the stars.
She called ; her voice no answer brought ;
She paused and bowed her head in thought.

The brightness of eternal morn
  Streamed through the portals on her face,
As though the flush of day, new-born,
  Forever glorified the place.
The singer raised her head and sang ;
Night listened, and the blue skies rang.

As softly as a wind-kissed rose
    Lets fall a petal to the ground,
So did the music, at its close,
    An echo drop of melting sound.
But no bright face drew near the bars
And smiled and listened with the stars.

On earth the singer's thrilling note
    Had held a breathless throng in awe;
And Fame her name in sunlight wrote
    Where passing thousands praising saw.
Now, none in all sweet Heaven came
To bow before that lofty name.

II.

Then did a maid draw near the place
    Whose brow might charm in Paradise.
The stars — those golden flowers that grace
    The dark lake of the midnight skies —
Were not more fair, with all their light,
Than her soft eyes, and not more bright.

Her tresses — gathered sunbeams — fell
    In rippling glory to her feet;
Her charms had bound men with their spell,
    But now none came her step to greet;

29

No bright eye gazed upon her there,
No angel spoke and called her fair.

III.

A monarch, dreaming dreams of gold,
    Drew near the jewelled gates divine,
But darkness closed about him cold,
    Scarce would the stars upon him shine ;
And, filled with shame, he bowed alone,
Dishonored, helpless, and unknown.

IV.

A woman poor, with patient face,
    And eyes made beautiful with trust,
With soul that never showed its grace
    Till freed from Time's frail house of dust,
Approached the shining portals now,
And lo ! God's glory bathed her brow.

Past was her bitter journey long.
    She touched the gate with trembling hand,
And through the portals broke a song
    That filled the night with music grand ;

Wide flew the gate; and, with glad face,
She entered that celestial place.

.   .   .   .   .

God reads the soul, and not the face;
    He hears the thoughts, and not the tongue.
In Heaven the features wear no grace
    Save that which round the spirit hung;
And only they are lovely seen
Whose lives on earth have noble been.

THE LOST DAY.

THE day is passed, the sun is gone;
The west is dark and sad and lone,
And shadows creep along the plain,
And through the shadows cries the rain,—
Cries low, and in the forest sobs,
Where like a heart each leaflet throbs.
O lonely south-winds, sighing so,
Have ye no reeds of hope to blow,
That thus the rustling weeds ye stir
Where Night drops blackness after her?

And ye, grim skies, why gaze ye down
With such a cold and brooding frown?
Beyond your clouds vast glories are:

The comet in his wheeling
   car —
The wandering ghost of
   some dead star, —
Glides brightly up the
   heavenly steep
Where golden planets shine and sleep:
Yet all these charms ye veil from sight,
And earth lies blind and pleads for light.
The day whose death ye mourn with tears
Will add no lustre to the years.
It *might* have shone with beauty warm;
It *was* a day of cloud and storm.
It *might* have healed with touch of gold
The blossoms drooping in the cold.

It *might* have decked the hills with flame,
And writ in heaven its golden name.
It *was* a day of darkness drear,
That came and ended in a tear.

But thou, O Night, hast grace thine own,
And wilt thou not for day atone?
Oh, clear these heavy glooms away,
And be a recompense for day!
Sing, sweet south-wind, the flowers among!
Shine forth, fair stars, in heaven hung!
And lo! from out the silent gloom
A new, bright day shall heaven illume,
Whose feet across the orient
Shall on their shining course be spent
To fill with joy the firmament.

God leaves the future fair and clean
To atone for all the past hath been,
And grants that from each sad distress
May rise and shine some blessedness.

THE NEW YEAR'S VISION.

THE sober clocks, from tower to tower,
Had pealed the solemn midnight hour,
And far across the frosty snow
The echoes died in music low;
When sudden, from the starlit skies,
With ruddy cheeks and gladdening eyes,
And lips like rosebuds pressed together
To keep them warm in frosty weather,
I saw the joyful new-born year
Descending with his hearty cheer.
His graceful form was bathed in light,
And 'round his face strange beauty bright
Where'er he passed made fair the night.
And ah! he had the fleetest wings
   That ever sprite or fairy knew;
The summer bird that soars and sings
   Would give his trill and warble too
To fly with pinions half so gay
As those that bore him on his way.

34

I looked again, and saw a throng
  Of tiny spirits floating after,
And half were singing a merry song,
  And half were joining in airy laughter.
As thick they came as flakes of snow,
  But bright as golden meteors swarming;
And, as I watched, it seemed as though
  The sparkling stars from heav'n were storming.

"What, ho! thou merry New Year's Elf,
  Come, pause a moment at my side,
And tell me all about yourself
  And all your fairy host," I cried.
He started softly at my word,
Then, poising lightly as a bird,
Descended quickly to my feet,
And said in words of music sweet,
"The Spirit of the Year am I,
And these, my playmates, hovering nigh,
Are Hours and Minutes, pure and gay,   ·
To bring good cheer to New Year's Day!"

Then all the listening hours and minutes,
As bright as stars and spry as linnets,
Caught hands in shining ring-around,
And danced and sang with skip and bound,

Till all the air with joy seemed ringing,
  And star seemed singing to sister star;
The very wind, more softly blowing,
  Seemed overflowing in music far.

And so the Hours and Minutes danced
  In revelry that never ceased
Till dawn's first beams like sly eyes glanced
  Between the curtains of the east.
Then said the New Year's Spirit to me:
  "These Hours, these Minutes, all are thine!
They come to comfort, to gladden thee,
  And make thy pathway fairer shine.
Be true, be patient, serve them well;
For though a while with thee they dwell
Yet must they flutter back this year,
And breathe the secret in God's ear
Of every thought thou gav'st them here!"

The Spirit vanished; but a song
Rang in my heart the whole day long.
That song, O world, I give to you:
"Be kind, be patient, just, and true,
For time will flutter back each year
And tell your secrets in God's ear."

36

POSSESSION.

THE golden pomp of stars, the dusk of night,
 The balm of blooming flowers, the dews that shine
 At silver dawn, each drop a crystalline,
The streams that sing themselves to sleep in light,
The sky, blue gate of day's high temple bright,
 The sun, God's brow half-seen, the hills divine
 With lavish blossoming, the sea's green shrine
Grand with eternal hymns, birds, cloudlets white, —
All these are mine! Man cannot sell and buy
 The works of God, and hide them in the clay!
 Wealth cannot buy the glory of the day!
I treasure more that bit of sunset sky
Than all yon mountain's wealth of hidden ore;
The gold I prize paves all fair heaven's floor.

A CHRISTMAS DREAM.

At midnight in the city streets I heard
  A carol sweet by passing voices sung.
  Over the drifted walls the music rung,
While round the window-pane the snows were stirred.

"The shepherds saw the star!" such was the word,
  Till each clear note from stormy distance sprung,
  And silence fell the city walls among,
As at the ended song of some night bird.

SWALLOW-FLIGHT.

O'ERHEAD the twittering swallows come and go,
  Those feathered spirits of the summer air.
  Not with the English lark their notes compare
That float among the listening clouds of snow,
Bathed in the tide of morning's purple glow;
  Not with the lark the world's wide praise they share,
  Yet each doth in his simple bosom bear
As glad a heart as ever lark may know.
  So if thy soul float but on swallows' wings,
While great men's spirits soar through fame like space,
  Know this: He hears thy simple twitterings
Who 'mong His bright works giveth thee a place,
  And on thy lowly pinions thou mayst float
  With just as pure a gladness in thy note.

THE SOUL'S DAY.

How like a flute-note on the dewy air
   The wild-bird's merry carol comes and goes!
   The East unfolds her colors like a rose
Whose heart is golden with the sun's warm glare.
What wonder that the bird-song is so rare!
   What wonder that the brook sings as it flows!
   The very earth, fresh from her night's repose,
Is wreathed in smiles at sight of dawn so fair.

O soul, this day is thine to imitate!
   Be thou a day clothed in the living light.
Rise to thy task, and, be it small or great,
   Shine on it till thy smile hath made it bright.
Smile, smile on all thy duties, and, behold!
Thy life, like day, shall walk in robes of gold.

And then I fell asleep, and dreamed I gazed
  Upon a manger where a child new-born
His pure, sweet eyes to mine with love upraised;
  And there I saw the shepherds, tired and worn.
And as with them I knelt in awe and praised,
  The sun shone in my eyes — 'twas Christmas morn!

CHASTISEMENT.

GOD's chastisements fall tenderly as snow,
  And come to clothe the suffering soul's offence
  With chaste white robes of perfect penitence,
That in the heart new germs of hope may grow.
God's face shines on us wheresoe'er we go,
  He knoweth how on all our good intents
  The frail dust of the mortal weighs, and hence
He shines to light us in our weal or woe.

'Tis not with flaming sword he drives us forth
  From out the sin and shame that cloud our praise;
For even while we err He is not wroth,
  Wounding with stripes the soul that disobeys.
Oh, I believe tears dim the dear Christ-eyes,
In heavenly sympathy for all our sighs.

THE BEAUTY OF AGE.

THE sun grows crimson, as the bright hours die.
    Along the shores the ripples softly beat,
    And towards that bourne where earth and heav'n
        meet,
The pink clouds drift in depths of smiling sky,
And gathering birds on tireless pinions fly;
    The time is like a happy lifetime sweet
    That stealeth calmly on its close to greet,
Mid all the tender charms that round it lie.

O Time! How softly must thou mould the years
    To wear that peace white age on man bestows!
    How glad must be thy touch, to leave such light
On life's horizon as the parting nears!
    If thus thou leadest on Death's lovely night,
    What wonders shall eternity disclose!

www.ingramcontent.com/pod-product-compliance
Lightning Source LLC
Chambersburg PA
CBHW061237260626
47172CB00003B/893